To my dad, thanks for everything! – S. S.

For my dad, Phillip 'Juggy' Julian – S. J.

Copyright © 2012 by Good Books, Intercourse, PA 17534
International Standard Book Number: 978-1-56148-744-8
Library of Congress Catalog Card Number: 2011031773

Text copyright © Steve Smallman 2012
Illustrations copyright © Sean Julian 2012
Original edition published in English by Little Tiger Press,
an imprint of Magi Publications, London, England, 2012
LTP/1400/0297/1011 • Printed in China

Library of Congress Cataloging-in-Publication Data
Smallman, Steve.
My dad / Steve Smallman ; [illustrated by] Sean Julian.
p. cm.
Summary: Everyone's dad is great at something and Little Bear decides
that, when he is big, he wants to be just like his dad.
ISBN 978-1-56148-744-8 (hardcover : alk. paper) [1. Stories in rhyme.
2. Father and child--Fiction. 3. Bears--Fiction.] I. Julian, Sean, ill. II. Title.
PZ8.3.S6358My 2012
[E]--dc23
2011031773

My Dad!

Steve Smallman   Sean Julian

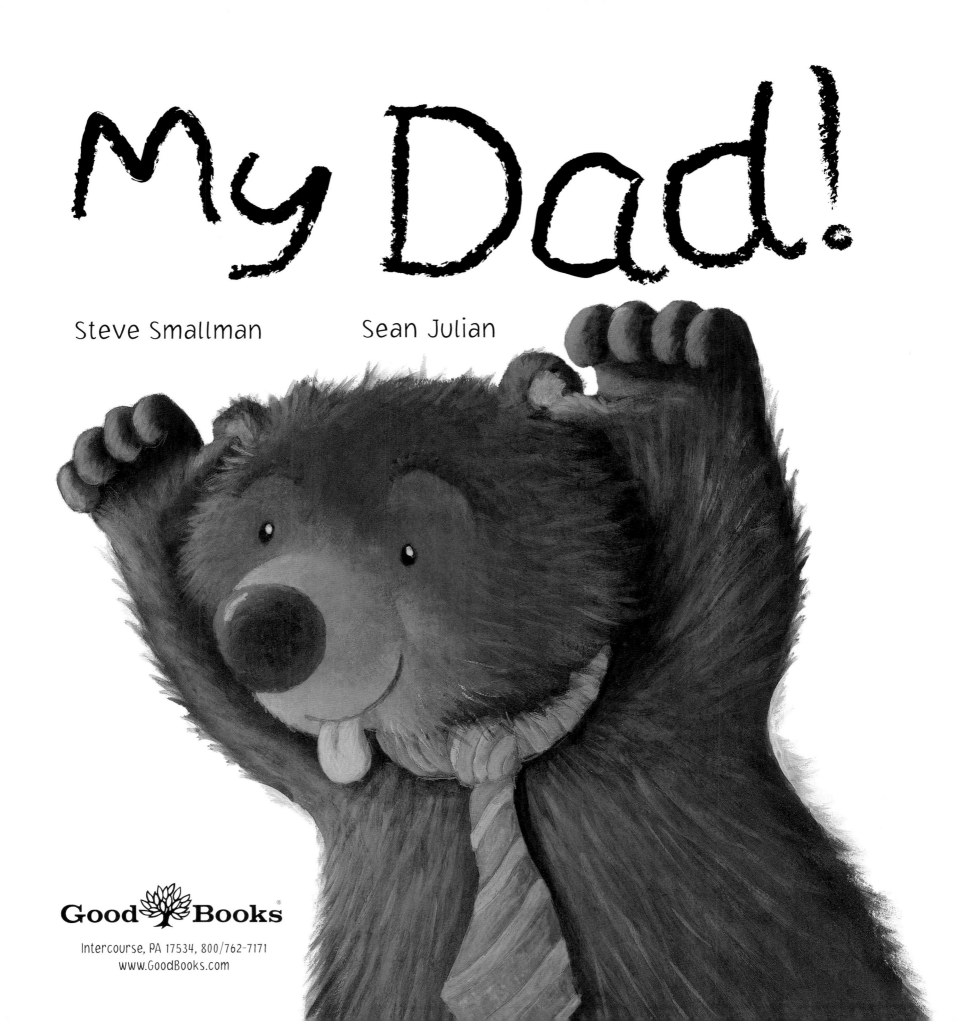

Good Books®

Intercourse, PA 17534, 800/762-7171
www.GoodBooks.com

Some dads just love to **snuggle** and cuddle.

Some dads join in when you **jump in a puddle!**

Some dads will run up
and down by your side,
Holding your bike till you
learn how to ride.

Some dads can cheer you up
when you're crying,

And hold you **so high** that you feel like you're flying!

Some dads will help you whatever you do.

TOOT!

Some dads will toot
and then say it was you!

Some dads build magical castles of sand,

Or make you feel safe
just by holding
your hand.

Some dads drink soda
and give you a slurp,
And then laugh out loud
when you do a big burp!

Some dads look **BIG** as a **GIANT** to you, And up on their shoulders you feel like one too!

Some dads get upset and start grumbling and stamping,

GRRRRRRRRR!

Just because they're kind
of hopeless at camping!

Some dads try hard but they really can't cook,

And some dads are just
great at reading a book.

Nobody's dad is like mine— and I'm glad.

When I'm big I want to be **just** *like* my dad!